Philip Hall likes me.
I reckon maybe.

by BETTE GREENE

Pictures by Charles Lilly

PUFFIN BOOKS

W9-ATJ-371

PUFFIN BOOKS

Published by the Penguin Group

Penguin Putnam Books for Young Readers,
345 Hudson Street, New York, New York 10014, U.S.A.
Penguin Books Ltd, 27 Wrights Lane, London W8 5TZ, England
Penguin Books Australia Ltd, Ringwood, Victoria, Australia
Penguin Books Canada Ltd, 10 Alcorn Avenue, Toronto, Ontario, Canada M4V 3B2
Penguin Books (N.Z.) Ltd, 182-190 Wairau Road, Auckland 10, New Zealand

Penguin Books Ltd, Registered Offices: Harmondsworth, Middlesex, England

First published in the United States of America by The Dial Press, 1974
Published by Puffin Books,
a member of Penguin Putnam Books for Young Readers, 1999

7 9 10 8 6

Text copyright © Bette Greene, 1974
Illustrations copyright © The Dial Press, 1974
All rights reserved

CIP IS AVAILABLE UPON REQUEST FROM THE LIBRARY OF CONGRESS.

Printed in the United States of America

Except in the United States of America, this book is sold subject to the condition that
it shall nor, by way of trade or otherwise, be lent, re-sold, hired out, or otherwise
circulated without the publisher's prior consent in any form of binding or cover
other than that in which it is published and without a similar condition
including this condition being imposed on the subsequent purchaser.